SATURDAY

TEXT: **IAN LENDLER** • ILLUSTRATIONS: **SERGE BLOCH**

A NEAL PORTER BOOK
ROARING BROOK PRESS
NEW YORK

It's Saturday!
A stay-at-home day!

Saturday means my parents don't go to work . . .

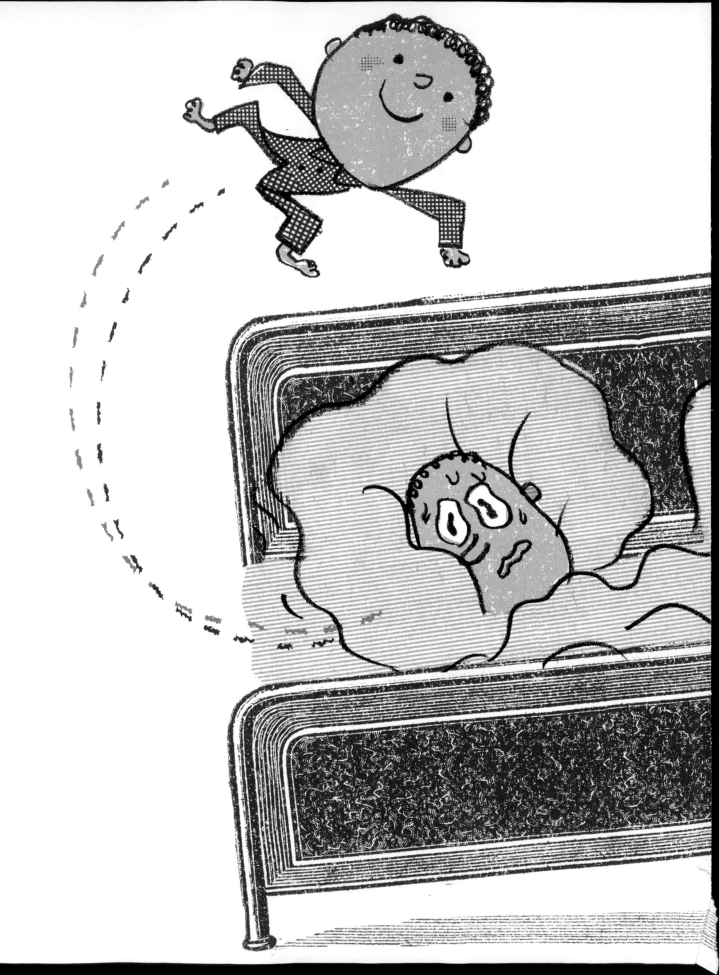

. . . so it's my job to start them early!

Saturday means family breakfast.

And family lunch.

And family dinner.

Saturday means Dad and I
finally have time to read
as many books as we like.

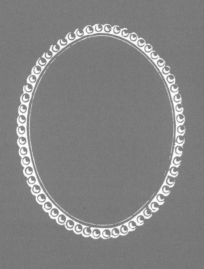

We like a lot of books.

Saturday means taking a rocket ship ride to the moon.

But sometimes our rocket runs out of gas.

Saturday means I have to defend the castle.

And take prisoners.

Saturday means working
on a top secret project
with my little brother.

Although it's so top secret we're not quite sure what it is.

Of course, Saturday doesn't
always mean staying home.

Sometimes I go to birthday parties,
so I have to look my best.

Mom and I don't always agree on what that means.

But my parents say that Saturday doesn't just mean having fun all day. It means other things too.

Like chores.

I hate chores.

Except when I get the chance to play superhero.

One of my chores is watering
my parents' garden . . .

. . . and sometimes my parents too.

Saturday also means Dad has to fix the house.

Then I have to fix Dad.

But my favorite part of Saturday is when there's nothing left to do.

Then I can just lie on the couch
with my dog, Frazzle . . .

And anyone else who wants to join in.

In fact, the only bad thing about Saturday
is that it has to end.

But that's okay.

Tomorrow is Sunday
and we can do it
all over again!

To Theo and Dylan —I.L.
To a week of seven Saturdays —S.B.

Text copyright © 2016 by Ian Lendler
Illustrations copyright © 2016 by Serge Bloch
A Neal Porter Book
Published by Roaring Brook Press
Roaring Brook Press is a division of Holtzbrinck Publishing Holdings Limited Partnership
175 Fifth Avenue, New York, New York 10010
The art for this book was made using pencil and digitally in Photoshop.
mackids.com

Library of Congress Cataloging-in-Publication Data

Names: Lendler, Ian, author. | Bloch, Serge, illustrator.
Title: Saturday / Ian Lendler, Serge Bloch.
Description: First edition. | New York : Roaring Brook Press, 2016. | "A Neal
  Porter Book." | Summary: "A boy tells us all the amazing things that
  happen on Saturday"– Provided by publisher.
Identifiers: LCCN 2015030532 | ISBN 9781596439658 (hardback)
Subjects: | CYAC: Family life–Fiction. | Play–Fiction. | BISAC: JUVENILE
  FICTION / Family / Parents. | JUVENILE FICTION / Family / Siblings. |
  JUVENILE FICTION / General.
Classification: LCC PZ7.L5382 Sat 2016 | DDC [E]–dc23
LC record available at http://lccn.loc.gov/2015030532

Our books may be purchased in bulk for promotional, educational, or business use. Please
contact your local bookseller or the Macmillan Corporate and Premium Sales Department
at (800) 221-7945 ext. 5442 or by e-mail at MacmillanSpecialMarkets@macmillan.com.

First edition 2016
Printed in China by Toppan Leefung Printing Ltd., Dongguan City, Guangdong Province

1 3 5 7 9 10 8 6 4 2